Prophets, Captives, and the Kingdom Rebuilt

Prophets, Captives, and the Kingdom Rebuilt
Copyright © 2008 by Lamp Post, Inc.

CIP applied for
ISBN: 978-0-310-71291-6

Requests for information should be addressed to: Grand Rapids, Michigan 49530

This book published in conjunction with Lamp Post, Inc.; 8367 Lemon Avenue, La Mesa, CA 91941

Series Editor: Bud Rogers
Managing Art Director: Merit Alderink

Printed in the United States of America

08 09 10 11 • 7 6 5 4 3 2 1

Prophets, Captives, and the Kingdom Rebuilt

2 Kings-Nehemiah

Series Editor: Bud Rogers
Edited by Brett Burner and JS Earls
Story by **Young Shin Lee**
Art by **Jung Sun Hwang**

ZONDERVAN.com/
AUTHORTRACKER
follow your favorite authors

SECOND KINGS
PART 2

PERFECT!

THE KINGDOM OF JUDAH

I -- AMAZIAH, GREAT KING OF JUDAH -- AND MY BRAVE ARMY OF JUDAH SHALL BE UNSTOPPABLE! WE EVEN HAVE THE ISRAELITE SOLDIERS TO HELP US.

NOW IS THE TIME TO CONQUER EDOM ONCE AND FOR ALL!

KNOCK! KNOCK!

KING AMAZIAH!

THAT IMBECILE!

KING AMAZIAH, THERE'S A PROPHET WAITING TO SPEAK WITH YOU.

OFFICE

Do not disturb King Amaziah!

BAM!

HOW MANY TIMES MUST I TELL YOU TO CALL ME "GREAT KING AMAZIAH"!?!

WHOOPS!

GREAT KING AMAZIAH! PLEASE FORGIVE ME --

STAND ON YOUR SILLY HAT IN MY OFFICE UNTIL I RETURN!

PLEASE RETURN THE ISRAELITE SOLDIERS. GOD WILL LET YOU DEFEAT EDOM WITHOUT ISRAEL'S SUPPORT.

WELL... IT'S ONLY EDOM. FINE, I'LL RETURN THEM RIGHT AWAY.

AS GOD PROMISED, KING AMAZIAH WON A GREAT VICTORY OVER EDOM.

LIKE I SAID, NO PROBLEMO!

WHAT SHOULD WE DO WITH OUR TEN THOUSAND PRISONERS?

TOSS 'EM OFF A CLIFF. SEE HOW MANY CAN FLY.

HUH? WHAT'S THAT?

IDOL OF EDOM

IT MUST BE THE IDOL EDOM SERVED.

IDOL?!?

LET'S TAKE IT TO JUDAH. YOU CAN NEVER HAVE TOO MANY GODS.

TO WHOM IT MAY CONCERN,

I, WHO AM AS BRAVE AS A LION, THE HERO OF THE CENTURY, DECLARE WAR ON YOU, JEHOASH, KING OF THE VERY WIMPY LAND OF ISRAEL.

YOURS TRULY, GREAT KING AMAZIAH

P.S: I MIGHT FORGIVE YOU IF YOU BOW BEFORE ME. MAYBE.

YOUR KING REALLY WROTE THIS?

YES. WHY?

HE CAN'T BE SERIOUS?

SEND HIM MY RESPONSE...

A THISTLE IN LEBANON SAID TO THE CEDAR IN LEBANON, 'GIVE YOUR DAUGHTER TO MY SON AS A WIFE.' THEN A WILD BEAST IN LEBANON PASSED BY AND TRAMPLED THE THISTLE.

????????? ????????

WHAT I MEAN IS THIS: YOU'VE DEFEATED EDOM AND YOUR HEART IS HIGH. ENJOY YOUR SUCCESS BUT STAY AT HOME. OTHERWISE, YOU WILL FALL... AND JUDAH WILL FALL WITH YOU.

... AND THAT'S WHAT THE KING OF ISRAEL SAID.

ARGH!

I, THE GREAT AMAZIAH, SHALL ACHIEVE ANOTHER HISTORIC VICTORY.

AND I, JEHOASH, WILL TEACH YOU THE DIFFERENCE BETWEEN ISRAEL AND EDOM.

SO JEHOASH WENT OUT TO FACE AMAZIAH AT BETH SHEMESH IN JUDAH.

LET'S RUMBLE! ROCK THEIR WORLD!

BUT...

OY VEY.

I CAPTURED HIS LOWNESS, THE NOT-SO-GREAT KING AMAZIAH.

JEHOASH, HEY BUD, I WAS JUST JOKIN' AROUND...

I'VE GOT TWO WORDS FOR YOU.

BE QUIET!

TEAR DOWN THE WALL OF JERUSALEM SO I MAY CLAIM THEIR GOLD, SILVER, AND TREASURES!

JERUSALEM

I CAN'T BELIEVE WE BOUGHT A HOUSE ON THE WALL!

DON'T THINK OF IT AS A HOLE. JUST THINK OF IT AS A REALLY BIG WINDOW.

THIS IS ALL AMAZIAH'S FAULT!

LET'S GET RID OF HIM!

WHUMP!

WHAT?

TREASON?

TIME FOR A VACATION!

ZOOOOM!

THOSE AGAINST KING AMAZIAH SENT MEN AFTER HIM AND KILLED HIM IN LACHISH.

I COULDA BEEN A CONTENDER... OH WELL.

NOW LET'S TURN OUR ATTENTION TO SOME OF THE PROPHETS -- JONAH, AMOS, AND HOSEA -- THOSE FROM THE TIME OF KING JEROBOAM, SON OF JEHOASH.

THE STORY OF JONAH

JONAH! JONAH!

WHAT? WHO'S THERE? WASSUP?

I AM GOD!

GOD?

YES, GOD?!?

ARISE. GO TO NINEVEH AND PREACH AGAINST IT BECAUSE ITS WICKEDNESS HAS COME UP BEFORE ME.

HMM...

LET ME READ MY GUIDE BOOK BEFORE I ACT.

WHY DON'T YOU JUST ZAP 'EM THEN?

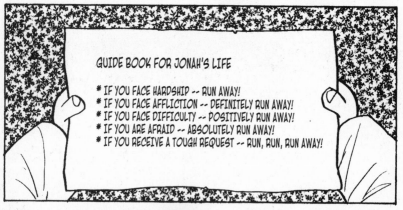

GUIDE BOOK FOR JONAH'S LIFE

* IF YOU FACE HARDSHIP -- RUN AWAY!
* IF YOU FACE AFFLICTION -- DEFINITELY RUN AWAY!
* IF YOU FACE DIFFICULTY -- POSITIVELY RUN AWAY!
* IF YOU ARE AFRAID -- ABSOLUTELY RUN AWAY!
* IF YOU RECEIVE A TOUGH REQUEST -- RUN, RUN, RUN AWAY!

NOW I KNOW WHAT I MUST DO...

RUN AWAY!!!

ZIP!

THE CITY OF JOPPA

IF I SAIL TO TARSHISH, THE LORD WON'T FOLLOW ME AND REQUEST ANYTHING FROM ME.

TARSHISH? YOU GOT IT, LITTLE BUDDY. WELCOME ABOARD!

VERY GOOD! LET'S DEPART!

WAIT!

YOU GOTTA PAY IN ADVANCE!

ARE YOU SURE THIS SHIP IS SAFE?

OF COURSE THIS SHIP IS SAFE! IT'S THE SAFEST SHIP IN THE MEDITERRANEAN!

OF COURSE, WE **COULD** HAVE TROUBLE IF WE RUN INTO AN ICEBERG.

YOU DO KNOW HOW TO **SWIM**, RIGHT?

I'LL JUST SIT BACK AND TAKE A LITTLE NAP.

SNOOORRRE!

JONAH! JONAH!

OH NO. NOT AGAIN.

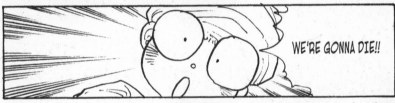

WE'RE GONNA DIE!!

I CAN'T SAIL IN THIS STORM! CALL ON YOUR GODS! MAYBE THEY'LL SAVE US!

GOD OF THE SEA! PLEASE FORGIVE US

GOD OF THE STORM! PLEASE STOP THIS!

BOOM!

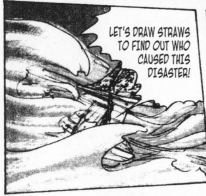

LET'S DRAW STRAWS TO FIND OUT WHO CAUSED THIS DISASTER!

ULP!

WHAT ARE YOU HIDING, JONAH?

NEMO

I DISOBEYED THE ONE TRUE GOD WHO MADE THE SEA AND THE LAND. THROW ME INTO THE SEA AND IT WILL BE CALMED FOR YOU.

I HATE TO LOSE A PAYING CUSTOMER.

LET'S WEATHER THIS STORM TOGETHER!

LATER...

KRRRACKT!

YOU DID SAY YOU CAN SWIM, RIGHT?

AS SOON AS JONAH WAS THROWN INTO THE SEA, THE SEA STOPPED RAGING.

A MOMENT OF SILENCE PLEASE.

ORCA

I SMELL SOMETHING YUMMY!

SPLOP!

THAT WAS TOTALLY DISGUSTING.

JONAH, GO TO NINEVEH AND PROCLAIM TO IT THE MESSAGE I GIVE YOU.

NO PROBLEM, I'LL GET RIGHT ON IT.

FORTY DAYS!

THE CITY OF NINEVEH

AFTER FORTY DAYS NINEVEH WILL BE DESTROYED!

WHAT'S HE BABBLING ABOUT?

WHAT'S THIS?!?

IT'S BEEN FORTY DAYS!
WHERE'S THE WRATH?
WHERE'S THE CARNAGE?!?

GOD MUST HAVE FORGIVEN
US BECAUSE WE ALL
TURNED TOWARD HIM!

O LORD! WHY DID YOU RESCUE THESE
SINFUL PEOPLE?

TAKE MY LIFE! I'M A COMPLETE AND UTTER FAILURE!

HMM... MAYBE I'LL SEE THE DESTRUCTION OF NINEVEH FROM HERE.

OUCH! IT'S TOO HOT!!!

STILL, I MUST WATCH. HMM... WHAT'S THIS?

IT'S A CUTE LITTLE PLANT.

SPR-RRR-RING!

WAHOO! GOTTA LOVE THE SHADE!

THE NEXT MORNING...

CHOMP! CHOMP!

WHO'S MAKING ALL THAT RACKET?

CHOMP! CHOMP!

OH NO YOU DON'T!!!

TOO LATE!

RIPT!

NO! A WORM ATE MY PLANT!

AAACK!

NO PLANT, NO SHADE... JUST KILL ME NOW!

SIZZLE!

SIZZLE!

JONAH, YOU ARE SO CONCERNED ABOUT A PLANT WHICH CAME AND WENT IN A DAY.

SHOULD I NOT BE CONCERNED WITH NINEVEH, WHERE THERE ARE OVER A HUNDRED AND TWENTY THOUSAND PEOPLE?

I'M SORRY, LORD. NOW, I UNDERSTAND.

THE END OF JONAH'S STORY

THE STORY OF AMOS

AMOS WAS A SHEPHERD FROM THE VILLAGE OF TEKOA IN JUDAH.

YES, I AM AMOS.

ONE DAY...

AMOS! AMOS!

YES, LORD?

GO TO ISRAEL WITH A MESSAGE.

I WILL DO AS YOU SAY.

HOW DARE HE? WHO DOES THAT SHEPHERD THINK HE IS? I'M THE PRIEST OF THIS TOWN!

I'M AMAZIAH!

.......!

THE KING?

NOT **THAT** AMAZIAH! HE'S DEAD!!! I'M THE PRIEST OF BETHEL!

AMOS, YOU'RE JUST A FORTUNE-TELLER! GO BACK TO JUDAH, IF YOU WANT TO LIVE!

I'M NOT A FORTUNE-TELLER OR A PROPHET. I AM ONLY A SHEPHERD. BUT GOD TOLD ME TO SHARE THESE WORDS WITH ISRAEL.

I SEE YOU'RE STILL HERE. JUDAH'S THAT WAY!

SINCE YOU DISOBEY GOD'S WILL, I WILL GIVE YOU HIS WORD.

YOUR WIFE WILL BECOME A HARLOT, YOUR CHILDREN WILL FALL BY THE SWORD, AND YOU WILL DIE IN A PAGAN COUNTRY!

HE FAINTED!

HE'S IN SHOCK.

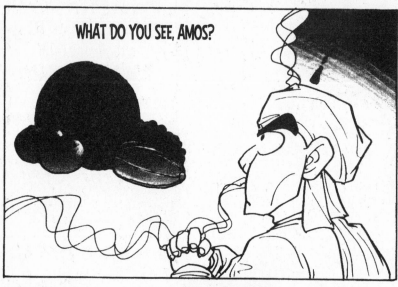

THEN THE LORD GOD OF HOSTS SPOKE TO AMOS...

WHAT DO YOU SEE, AMOS?

I SEE RIPE FRUIT.

THE TIME IS RIPE FOR MY PEOPLE ISRAEL; I WILL SPARE THEM NO LONGER.

IN THAT DAY THE SONGS IN THE TEMPLE WILL TURN TO WAILING.

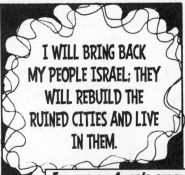
O LORD! THEN WILL ISRAEL PERISH FOREVER?

I WILL BRING BACK MY PEOPLE ISRAEL; THEY WILL REBUILD THE RUINED CITIES AND LIVE IN THEM.

THE END OF AMOS'S STORY

THE STORY OF HOSEA

THE WORD OF THE LORD CAME TO HOSEA DURING THE DAYS OF JEROBOAM WHEN ISRAEL'S PEOPLE WERE CORRUPTED BY WORSHIPING IDOLS.

HIYA, I'M HOSEA.

HOSEA! GO AND MARRY AN UNFAITHFUL WOMAN AND HAVE CHILDREN.

WHAT?

BUT THERE ARE SO MANY NICE GIRLS, LORD!

GOMER?

SHE'S OUT WITH ONE OF HER HUNDREDS OF BOYFRIENDS.

OKAY. WELL, I, UH...

WHAT A GEEK!

WELL, UH, SIR, I'D LIKE TO MARRY YOUR DAUGHTER GOMER.

?

HA! FINALLY!

I DON'T WANT TO KEEP YOU TWO LOVEBIRDS WAITING, SO LET'S SKIP THE WEDDING CEREMONY... AND THE HONEYMOON SINCE IT COSTS SO MUCH.

SIGN AT THE BOTTOM!

** MARRIAGE LICENSE **

I SIGNED IT. YIPPEE.

WHAT'S MOM GONNA SAY?

CRINKLE! CRINKLE!

I'VE DREAMED OF THIS DAY FOR SO LONG!

PLEASE MAKE MY ADORABLE DAUGHTER HAPPY.

DON'T WORRY ABOUT YOUR MOTHER. YOU KIDS HAVE A NICE LIFE TOGETHER!

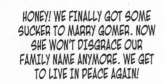
HONEY! WE FINALLY GOT SOME SUCKER TO MARRY GOMER. NOW SHE WON'T DISGRACE OUR FAMILY NAME ANYMORE. WE GET TO LIVE IN PEACE AGAIN!

WHAT?!? WHO TOOK HER?

SOME GUY FROM ISRAEL. I FEEL SORRY FOR HIM. BUT NOT THAT SORRY.

SINCE I GOT MARRIED, SOME STRANGE THINGS HAVE BEEN HAPPENING.

RING! RING!

A LOT OF LATE NIGHT PHONE CALLS WITH PEOPLE HANGING UP WITHOUT SAYING ANYTHING...

HELLO?

CLICK!

HOWEVER, IF GOMER ANSWERS...

YES... HEE, HEE...NINE O'CLOCK...

AND IF I ASK HER ABOUT THE CALLS...

WHY DO YOU HAVE TO KNOW EVERYTHING ALL THE TIME? YOU'RE A CONTROL FREAK!

I THOUGHT I WAS OVERREACTING, BUT ONE DAY...

DOES MADAME GOMER LIVE HERE?

MADAME GOMER?

WHO ARE YOU?

MUFFIN... STUD MUFFIN.

AND THEN...

ALTHOUGH I TRIED EVERYTHING TO SAVE OUR MARRIAGE, I FAILED. I STARTED TO COMPLAIN TO GOD.

LAST YEAR'S DISHES

BUT I STILL HOPED WE COULD STAY TOGETHER.

NOTHING'S CHANGED!

THEN I HAD AN IDEA...

FIRST OBSTACLE: BARBED WIRE!

SECOND OBSTACLE: HIGH WALL!

THIS'LL KEEP HER IN!

BUT SOME TIME AFTER I FINISHED...

I LOOK AT IT THIS WAY...

... EVERYONE FACES VARIOUS OBSTACLES IN THEIR LIVES.

BUT, WE MUST OVERCOME THAT WHICH HINDERS US.

EVEN BARBED WIRE...

... AND HIGH WALLS!

WHOOPS!

THUD!!

WE HAVE TO GO OUR OWN WAY.

LIMP
LIMP

ARGH!

I FINALLY GAVE UP.

GOMER DIDN'T COME BACK HOME.

TIME PASSED...

HOSEA! HOSEA!

YES, LORD?

GO TO GOMER AND BRING HER BACK. EVEN THOUGH SHE HAS TURNED AWAY FROM YOU, BRING HER BACK.

LOVE HER AS I LOVE THE ISRAELITES.

HOSEA!

Y-YES?

WHY ARE YOU NOT OBEYING ME?

WHY SHOULD I BRING HER BACK? SHE ONLY WANTS OTHER MEN.

WHY DO YOU THINK I HAD YOU MARRY A WOMAN LIKE HER?

TO SHOW US THE IMPORTANCE OF MARRIAGE?

IT WAS TO SHOW YOU MY FRUSTRATION WITH ISRAEL.

I LOVED ISRAEL AS MY WIFE, BUT SHE BETRAYED ME AND LOVED OTHERS. DO YOU SEE HOW FRUSTRATED I AM?

THE END OF HOSEA'S STORY

ALL RIGHT, NOW LET'S GET BACK TO THE HISTORY OF THE SOUTHERN KINGDOM OF JUDAH AND THE NORTHERN KINGDOM OF ISRAEL.

UZZIAH, WHO SUCCEEDED HIS FATHER AMAZIAH -- THE KING, NOT THE PRIEST -- AT THE AGE OF SIXTEEN, RULED JUDAH FOR FIFTY-TWO YEARS.

HE WAS CALLED AZARIAH WHEN HE WAS YOUNG, THEN UZZIAH WHEN HE BECAME KING.

EARLY ON, HE WAS ASSISTED BY THE PROPHET ZECHARIAH AND FOLLOWED THE WILL OF GOD...

AFTER THE DEATH OF ZECHARIAH, JUDAH BECAME WEALTHY, AND KING UZZIAH GREW PRIDEFUL.

OLD KING UZZIAH.

AH, THE GOOD OLD DAYS.

I DID MANY GREAT THINGS FOR GOD! I SHOULD GO TO THE TEMPLE AND BURN SOME INCENSE.

GASP!

GOD HAS PUNISHED THE KING BY TURNING HIM INTO A LEPER!

EVENTUALLY KING UZZIAH DIED, AND BECAUSE OF HIS LEPROSY HE WASN'T BURIED WITH HIS FOREFATHERS.

AHAZ, THE GRANDSON OF UZZIAH, LATER BECAME THE NEW KING OF JUDAH.

MY LIFE'S GOAL IS TO FOLLOW BAAL.

MY KING. THE PROPHET OF BAAL IS HERE.

TELL ME, PROPHET OF BAAL, WHY IS THERE FAMINE IN THE LAND?

O GREAT BAAL, PLEASE GIVE YOUR KING AN ANSWER!

WHAT DID BAAL SAY?

THIS FAMINE IS A TEST FROM BAAL!

YOU MUST SACRIFICE ONE SON TO BAAL IMMEDIATELY!

SO AHAZ, THE KING OF JUDAH, SACRIFICED HIS SON TO BAAL, AND GOD'S PUNISHMENT BEGAN.

ARAM INVADED JUDAH AND KILLED TENS OF THOUSANDS AND TOOK TENS OF THOUSANDS MORE AS SLAVES!

ISRAEL INVADED JUDAH TOO AND KILLED OVER ONE HUNDRED THOUSAND SOLDIERS.

THEY ALSO TOOK TWO HUNDRED THOUSAND WOMEN AND CHILDREN AS SLAVES.

WAIT!

STOP!

OH! WHAT ARE YOU DOING HERE, PROPHET ODED?

GOD SENT THE ARMY OF ISRAEL TO PUNISH THE SINFUL JUDAH!

WHY ARE YOU BRINGING BACK YOUR OWN PEOPLE AS SLAVES?

YOU WILL BE PUNISHED BY GOD IF YOU DO NOT RETURN THEM!

ISRAEL RETURNED THE CAPTURED PEOPLE OF JUDAH AFTER FEEDING AND CLOTHING THEM.

BE CAREFUL.

WE WILL PROVIDE PROTECTION ALL THE WAY TO JERICHO.

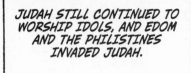

JUDAH STILL CONTINUED TO WORSHIP IDOLS, AND EDOM AND THE PHILISTINES INVADED JUDAH.

I WILL AVENGE JUDAH!

JUDAH IS NOTHING!

I'LL ASK FOR HELP FROM MIGHTY ASSYRIA.

KING AHAZ EVEN GAVE THE KING OF ASSYRIA MANY TREASURES FROM THE TEMPLE, BUT IT DIDN'T HELP.

ASSYRIA TRICKED ME!

THE GODS OF ARAM MUST BE STRONG! I'LL WORSHIP THE GODS OF ARAM!

NOW HEAR THIS! NAIL GOD'S TEMPLE SHUT AND ONLY WORSHIP THE GOD OF ARAM!

WHEN AHAZ DIED, HE WASN'T BURIED WITH THE OTHER KINGS EITHER.

WHAT DID I DO WRONG?

WHEN AHAZ RULED JUDAH AND WORSHIPED IDOLS, ISRAEL WAS RULED BY KING HOSHEA.

I AM KING HOSHEA -- NOT TO BE CONFUSED WITH THE PROPHET HOSEA!

I LIKE THIS TREE!

BUILD A STATUE OF ASHERAH UNDER THAT TREE!

GOD'S NOT GONNA LIKE THAT.

YOU DARE TO DEFY ME? YOU DIE!

I'M KING SHALMANESER OF ASSYRIA. I THINK I'LL INVADE ISRAEL!

WHEN ISRAEL'S SINS BECAME GREAT, GOD MADE SHALMANESER WANT TO INVADE ISRAEL.

NOOO! ACK! CRUNCH!!

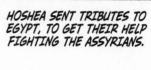

TIME PASSED AND KING SHALMANESER DIED. HIS SON SARGON BECAME THE NEW KING.

NOW'S MY CHANCE!

HOSHEA SENT TRIBUTES TO EGYPT, TO GET THEIR HELP FIGHTING THE ASSYRIANS.

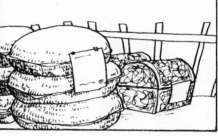

HOW DARE THE ISRAELITES! I'LL CRUSH THEM!!!

ISRAEL WAS CRUSHED

HELP ME, EGYPT!

KING HOSHEA

EGYPT IS BUSY WITH OUR OWN PROBLEMS!

KING HOSHEA WAS CAPTURED AND PUT IN PRISON.

CAN YOU GIVE ME SOME FOOD?

THE CITY OF SAMARIA WAS THEN SURROUNDED BY THE ASSYRIAN ARMY.

SARGON THE KING OF ASSYRIA

THE CITY OF SAMARIA

MOUSE TRAP

ISRAEL LASTED FOR THREE YEARS, BUT FINALLY FELL TO THE ASSYRIAN ARMY. THE KINGDOM OF ISRAEL, WHICH BEGAN WITH JEROBOAM OVER TWO HUNDRED YEARS AGO, WAS DESTROYED.

THE KINGS AND PROPHETS OF ISRAEL

KINGS	PROPHETS	PERIOD
JEROBOAM I		930-909 B.C.
BAASHA		908-886 B.C.
OMRI		885-874 B.C.
	ELIJAH	875-848 B.C.
AHAB		874-853 B.C.
JORAM		852-841 B.C.
	ELISHA	848-797 B.C.
JEHU		841-814 B.C.
JEHOAHAZ		814-798 B.C.
	JONAH	800-750 B.C.
JEHOASH		798-782 B.C.
JEROBOAM II		793-753 B.C.
	AMOS	760-750 B.C.
ZECHARIAH		753-752 B.C.
SHALLUM		752 B.C.
MENAHEM		752-742 B.C.
	HOSEA	750-715 B.C.
PEKAH		752-732 B.C.
PEKAHIAH		742-740 B.C.
HOSHEA		732-722 B.C.

ISAIAH WAS BORN IN JUDAH, THE SON OF A PROMINENT FAMILY.

YOU GOT IT, I'M ISAIAH!

WHEN KING UZZIAH DIED OF LEPROSY...

WHAT'S GOING TO HAPPEN TO THE FAITH OF JUDAH NOW THAT UZZIAH DIED?

OH!

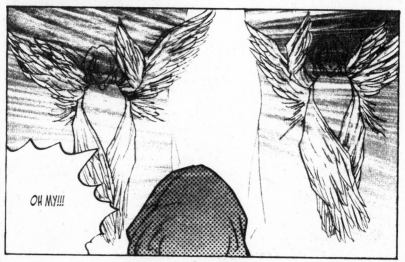

OH MY!!!

CRUSH THE IDOLS AND MELT THE SNAKE MOSES MADE!

HI-YAH!

THE BRONZE SNAKE MOSES MADE WASN'T MEANT TO BE AN IDOL, BUT OVER TIME IT WAS WORSHIPED AS AN IDOL. (PLEASE SEE THE MANGA BIBLE BOOK 2, PAGES 16 - 18 FOR FURTHER DETAILS)

I WAS HEALED AFTER I LOOKED AT THE SNAKE!

ME TOO!

I AM A POLE-VAULTER; HAVE YOU SEEN MY POLE?

NODE. SORRY!

WOULD IT WORK ON MY STOMACHACHE?

GOD BLESSED HEZEKIAH AND MADE JUDAH LARGE AND POWERFUL.

WE RETURN FROM CRUSHING THE PHILISTINES.

GIVE THANKS TO GOD FIRST!

FROM KICKING IDOLS

SOON, JUDAH HAD TROUBLE...

JUDAH IS MIGHTY?

GATHER MY ARMY! LET'S GO!

WHAT? ISRAEL IS DESTROYED?!?

AND KING SARGON'S SON SENNACHERIB IS COMING?!?

AS KING SENNACHERIB REACHED JERUSALEM...

I'M REMINDED OF MY FATHER WHO DESTROYED ISRAEL.

WE'RE REMINDED OF ISRAEL'S DESTRUCTION.

HEY, YOU! GO AND SCARE THEM A LITTLE.

YES, SIR!

AL-WAYS! I WILL ALWAYS LO-OVE YOU!

TO-DAY AND TO-MORROW! AL-WAYS!

THIS IS NO TIME FOR SINGING!

SORRY! I DON'T KNOW WHERE THAT CAME FROM...

AN EXTRA WHO WANTS TO BE IN ONE MORE PANEL.

WHAT? WE'RE BEING ATTACKED BY AN UNKNOWN ARMY?!?

NONE CAN DEFEAT OUR ASSYRIAN ARMY! CRUSH THEM!!!

AUGH!

HEL-LP!

NOOOO!!!

THE NEXT MORNING...

WHAT HAPPENED? NO ENEMY BODIES? ONLY ONE HUNDRED AND EIGHTY-FIVE THOUSAND OF OURS?

THIS IS AWFUL! LET'S HURRY BACK TO ASSYRIA!!!

EVEN MORE DISASTER WAS WAITING FOR KING SENNACHERIB IN ASSYRIA...

HE WAS KILLED BY HIS SONS WHEN HE RETURNED.

WHERE DID I GO WRONG?

I AM NOW KING AFTER KILLING OUR FATHER!

WHAT? NO, I AM NOW KING!

WHO WOULD DARE OPPOSE THE ARMY OF THE ONE TRUE GOD?

ONE DAY... OOOOH, I CAN'T GET UP. MY BODY IS SO SORE IT'S KILLING ME!

KING HEZEKIAH, YOU WILL DIE.

WHAT!?! WHY WOULD YOU SAY SOMETHING LIKE THAT, ISAIAH?

GOD SAID TO PUT YOUR HOUSE IN ORDER BECAUSE YOU WILL DIE SOON.

I MUST BE GOING NOW.

OH! GOD, PLEASE SAVE ME!

REMEMBER HOW I TRIED TO LIVE MY LIFE FOR YOU?

ISAIAH, GIVE HEZEKIAH A NEW MESSAGE.

YOU WILL LIVE.

WHAT!?! DON'T PLAY WITH ME!

GOD SAW YOUR TEARS AND SAID THE FOLLOWING...

"THREE DAYS FROM NOW YOU WILL GO UP TO THE TEMPLE OF THE LORD. I WILL ADD FIFTEEN YEARS TO YOUR LIFE."

YOU'LL BE HEALED IF YOU USE A MIXTURE OF FIGS.

IS THERE A SIGN THAT I'LL BE HEALED?

LOOK OUTSIDE.

SHALL THE SUNDIAL TURN FORWARD OR BACKWARD TEN DEGREES?

MOVING THE DAY BACKWARD IS HARDER.

JUDAH'S SUNDIAL CLOCK

THERE, YOU SEE?

GOD TURNED BACK THE CLOCK!

AND SO, KING HEZEKIAH WENT TO THE TEMPLE, WORSHIPED GOD, AND LIVED FIFTEEN MORE YEARS.

REMEMBER KIDS; TRUST GOD AND PRAY!

WHEN KING HEZEKIAH DIED, HIS SON MANASSEH BECAME KING AT THE AGE OF TWELVE.

ME MANASSEH!

I AM REBUILDING THE TEMPLE OF BAAL MY FATHER DESTROYED!

I'M GOING TO PUT A STATUE OF ASHERAH IN GOD'S TEMPLE!

I'LL EVEN SACRIFICE MY OWN SON TO THE IDOL!

KING MANASSEH! DON'T YOU FEAR GOD? HOW DARE YOU DO THESE THINGS!

KILL GOD'S PROPHETS, ESPECIALLY ISAIAH!

AND SO, THE PROPHET ISAIAH WAS PUT TO DEATH.

* TOO HORRIBLE TO DRAW.

MANASSEH'S WORSHIPING OF IDOLS GREW WORSE AND GOD SENT THE ASSYRIAN ARMY TO JUDAH.

HERE WE COME!!!

KING MANASSEH WAS CAPTURED AND TAKEN TO BABYLON AS PRISONER.

UNHAND ME!

ULP!

DON'T BE LAZY! PUT MORE PICTURES IN OR YOU'RE FIRED!!!

OKAY, FINE.

INSIDE A BABYLONIAN JAIL...

I'M HERE BECAUSE I WORSHIPED IDOLS!

GOD, PLEASE LET ME LIVE!

I WILL WORSHIP YOU AND YOU ALONE!

HERE'S A THOUGHT...

WHY SHOULD I KEEP MANASSEH? HE'S JUST ANOTHER MOUTH TO FEED.

SEND MANASSEH HOME BUT WARN HIM THAT HE'LL BE KILLED IF HE DOESN'T OBEY US!

NOW LEAVING BABYLON

I'M FREE!

LIMP. LIMP.

THE KING HAS CHANGED!

WHO WOULD'VE THOUGHT HE WOULD ORDER ALL THE IDOLS DESTROYED?

WE NEED DIFFICULT TIMES IN LIFE TO UNDERSTAND WHAT'S REALLY IMPORTANT.

CHUNK!

Idol Destruction Sight

Pardon our Oust

I SAY IT'S NOW TIME TO BUILD THE ALTARS OF GOD EVEN BIGGER!

KING MANASSEH RULED FOR FIFTY-SIX YEARS, THE LONGEST IN THE HISTORY OF JUDAH.

BECAUSE I TURNED AND WORSHIPED ONLY GOD.

WHEN KING MANASSEH DIED, HIS SON AMON BECAME KING, BUT AMON WORSHIPED IDOLS AND ONLY RULED FOR TWO YEARS.

IT'S BETTER TO WORSHIP MANY GODS.

THE PEOPLE MADE AMON'S SON JOSIAH THE NEW KING.

WHO SHOULD I BE LIKE?

KING JOSIAH WAS AS HOLY AS KING DAVID. HE STARTED A RELIGIOUS REVOLUTION AND ELIMINATED ALL THE IDOLS IN THE LAND IN SIX YEARS.

SOMEBODY TALKIN' ABOUT ME? MY EAR ITCHES.

I'M PROUD EVERY TIME I SEE HIM.

IDOLZ

JOSIAH'S RELIGIOUS REVOLUTION DID NOT END IN JUDAH; THEY ALSO EXPANDED INTO NORTHERN ISRAEL.

THAT'S WHY NORTHERN ISRAEL WAS DESTROYED.

THE TOMB OF THE PROPHETS WHO WORSHIPED JEROBOAM'S GOLDEN CALF!

TOMB OF PROPHETS

DIG UP ALL THE BONES, GRIND THEM, AND SPREAD THE ASHES OVER THE ALTAR.

IT WAS PROPHESIED THREE HUNDRED YEARS EARLIER THAT THE BONES OF THE PROPHETS WOULD BE BURNED ON THE UNCLEAN ALTAR.

I DREW THAT FOR YOU BACK IN VOLUME 4, PAGE 52. CHECK IT OUT.

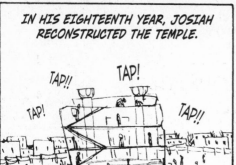

IN HIS EIGHTEENTH YEAR, JOSIAH RECONSTRUCTED THE TEMPLE.

TAP!!
TAP!
TAP!
TAP!!

HEY, WHAT'S THIS BOOK?

WHAT ARE YOU DOING WITH THE BOOK OF THE LAW?!?

WHAT IS THIS?

THE BOOK OF THE LAW!

THAT'S THE BOOK OF THE LAW?

YES, YOUR MAJESTY...

... IT WAS DISCOVERED DURING THE RECONSTRUCTION OF THE TEMPLE, AND I WAS TOLD TO BRING IT TO YOU.

PLEASE READ IT TO ME.

OOOOH!!

WHY ARE YOU CRYING AND TEARING YOUR ROBE WHILE I'M READING THIS BOOK?

YOU DON'T KNOW?!? YOU JUST READ THE WORDS OF GOD AND HIS WARNINGS AGAINST THOSE WHO DISOBEY HIS COMMANDS!

WHAT'S GOING TO HAPPEN TO THOSE IN JUDAH WHO DON'T FOLLOW GOD'S COMMANDS? IS THERE ANYONE WHO KNOWS WHAT WILL HAPPEN TO THIS COUNTRY?

WELL, THERE'S A WISE PROPHETESS NAMED HULDAH...

GO. FIND HULDAH NOW AND ASK HER WHAT GOD'S WILL IS!

IT IS AS THE BOOK OF THE LAW SAYS. MANY IN JUDAH HAVE DISOBEYED THE LAW AND HAVE WORSHIPED IDOLS. FOR THAT, A TERRIBLE JUDGMENT WILL BE HANDED DOWN.

HOWEVER, BECAUSE GOD SAW KING JOSIAH'S TEARS, THIS JUDGMENT WILL COME AFTER HIS DEATH.

Doo.

AND THAT'S WHAT SHE SAID.

JOSIAH GATHERED ALL THE PEOPLE, READ THE BOOK OF THE LAW, AND TOLD THEM TO ONLY FOLLOW GOD.

THE DISCOVERY OF THE BOOK OF THE LAW WAS THE HIGHEST POINT IN JOSIAH'S RELIGIOUS REVOLUTION.

HOWEVER, THE PEOPLE OF JUDAH STILL WORSHIPED IDOLS.

I MUST WORSHIP IDOLS. IT'S A FAMILY TRADITION!

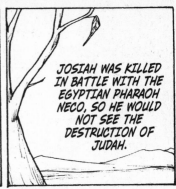

JOSIAH WAS KILLED IN BATTLE WITH THE EGYPTIAN PHARAOH NECO, SO HE WOULD NOT SEE THE DESTRUCTION OF JUDAH.

WHEN KING JOSIAH DIED, HIS SON JEHOAHAZ BECAME KING.

THEY SAY I HAVE A TERRIBLE TEMPER... AND THAT MAKES ME MAD!!!

PHARAOH NECO INVADED JUDAH, AND CAPTURED KING JEHOAHAZ, WHO DIED IN CAPTIVITY.

THAT'S NOT FAIR! I ONLY RULED FOR THREE MONTHS!!

I ONLY DREW HIM. WHY AM I A PRISONER?

PHARAOH NECO THEN MADE JEHOAHAZ'S OLDER BROTHER, ELIAKIM, KING.

ELIAKIM, YOU SHALL BE CALLED JEHOIAKIM, AND YOU SHALL RULE JUDAH! IN RETURN, GIVE ME GOLD. LOTS OF GOLD.

NO PROBLEMO, NECO.

JERUSALEM

ALL RIGHT! WE'LL ESCAPE THE CONTROL OF BABYLON BY SIDING WITH EGYPT!

HOW DARE JEHOIAKIM BETRAY ME JUST BECAUSE WE LOST ONE LITTLE BATTLE TO EGYPT!

MARCH! SEND THE ARMIES OF CHALDEA, ARAM, MOAB, AND AMMON TO DESTROY JUDAH!

JUDAH WAS DESTROYED AND THE PEOPLE OF JUDAH WERE TAKEN TO BABYLON AS SLAVES.

BEFORE YOU WERE BORN I SET YOU APART, AND NOW YOU WILL BE MY PROPHET!

O GOD, I'M ONLY A KID AND I DON'T SPEAK VERY WELL.

DO NOT BE AFRAID, FOR I AM WITH YOU.

NOW I HAVE PUT MY WORDS IN YOUR MOUTH. GO AND DELIVER MY MESSAGE!

WHAT DID YOU SEE, JEREMIAH?

A POT OF BOILING WATER WAS JUST ABOUT TO SPILL FROM NORTH TO SOUTH.

SOON, FROM THE NORTH, BABYLON WILL DESTROY JUDAH!

TURN FROM EVIL! GOD SAYS IF WE DON'T RETURN TO HIM, JUDAH WILL BE DESTROYED BY AN INVASION FROM THE NORTH!

AT A POTTER'S WORKSHOP...

ARE YOU HERE TO BUY SOME JARS?

NO, I'M JUST HERE TO WATCH.

THERE'S NOTHING TO SEE BUT THESE JARS I'M MAKING.

THE PEOPLE OF JUDAH ARE LIKE CLAY IN A POTTER'S HAND.

LET'S SEE IF THE POTS ARE READY.

YOU'RE FREE, JEREMIAH!

THE NEXT DAY...

BUT WE'LL KILL YOU IF YOU SAY SUCH THINGS AGAIN!

GOD WILL NOT CALL YOU "PASHHUR" ANYMORE, BUT "MAGOR-MISSABIB" SINCE YOU ARE A TERROR TO YOURSELF AND YOUR FRIENDS.

YOU WILL SEE THE HORRIBLE DESTRUCTION OF JUDAH BECAUSE OF YOUR FALSE PROPHECY!

JUDAH'S KING ZEDEKIAH

I CAN'T JUST SIT HERE AND BE UNDER THE RULE OF BABYLON!

IT'S TIME TO REPAY KING NEBUCHADNEZZAR, AND I CAN DO IT WITH EGYPT'S HELP!

THIS IS OUR CHANCE TO REPAY BABYLON!

THIS TIME WE'LL BE FREE FROM BABYLON FOR SURE!

LET'S FIGHT!

ARE YOU CRAZY? DO YOU WANT TO DIE?

HIM AGAIN? HE'S SUCH A DOWNER!

GOD PLACED KING NEBUCHADNEZZAR AS A RULER OVER US. THE ONLY WAY WE'LL SURVIVE IS TO LIVE UNDER HIS RULE.

WHEN YOU ARE FREED FROM BONDS OF WOOD, YOU WILL BE PUT IN BONDS OF IRON!

I DON'T WANT TO HEAR IT ANYMORE! THROW JEREMIAH IN JAIL, AND WE'LL GO FIGHT BABYLON.

WHAT? JUDAH BETRAYED US? CRUSH THEM!!!

WHEN FACING DANGER FROM BABYLON, ZEDEKIAH FREED SLAVES TO FIGHT AND ASKED FOR HELP FROM EGYPT.

I JUST CONVENIENTLY RECALLED THAT WE'RE NOT TO ENSLAVE OUR OWN PEOPLE.

WITH THE HELP OF THE EGYPTIAN ARMY, THE THREAT OF BABYLON WAS AVOIDED.

WE JUST DON'T WANT BABYLON TO BECOME MORE POWERFUL.

WITH THE THREAT ENDED, ZEDEKIAH ENSLAVED THE FORMER SLAVES AGAIN.

WHAT EQUALITY? ONCE A SLAVE, ALWAYS A SLAVE. SLAVE FREEDOM IS REVOKED!

THE KING OF EGYPT WON'T RETURN, BUT THE ARMY OF BABYLON WILL RETURN AND BURN THE CITY!

THAT JEREMIAH... TOSS HIM IN THE DUNGEONS!

I FEEL ODD ABOUT IMPRISONING JEREMIAH... AM I DOING SOMETHING WRONG?

SHUFFLE!

SHUFFLE!

GO GET JEREMIAH AND BRING HIM HERE.

WE'LL SEE HOW LONG YOU LAST IN THIS SEWER HOLE.

GO AHEAD AND PROPHESY ALL YOU WANT NOW!

JEREMIAH! PROPHET JEREMIAH!

I'M THE KING'S SERVANT. HE SENT ME TO SAVE YOU. TIE THIS ROPE AROUND YOU!

I NEVER WANTED TO KILL YOU. GO, HIDE YOURSELF IN THE CITY.

MY KING, EVEN NOW YOU AND YOUR CITY CAN BE SAVED IF YOU WILL ONLY SURRENDER TO BABYLON.

BUT KING ZEDEKIAH DIDN'T LISTEN, AND FINALLY, IN THE NINTH YEAR OF HIS REIGN, KING NEBUCHADNEZZAR'S ARMY SURROUNDED JERUSALEM.

KING ZEDEKIAH HELD OUT FOR EIGHTEEN MONTHS, BUT JERUSALEM FINALLY FELL TO THE BABYLONIANS.

WE'RE FINISHED! THEY'RE THROUGH!

THEY'RE THROUGH? WHO'S THROUGH?

THE BABYLONIANS HAVE BROKEN THROUGH THE CASTLE WALL AND THEY'RE RUSHING IN! WE'RE DOOMED!!!

WHERE ARE YOU GOING?

ZOOM!

I'VE GOT THINGS TO DO...

... AND PLACES TO GO!!!

KING ZEDEKIAH WAS CAPTURED BY KING NEBUCHADNEZZAR. HIS FAMILY AND THE NOBLES OF JUDAH WERE DESTROYED. MOST OF THE PEOPLE OF JERUSALEM WERE EXILED TO BABYLON, BUT JEREMIAH AND A SMALL REMNANT WERE LEFT BEHIND.

THE KINGS AND PROPHETS OF JUDAH

KINGS	PROPHETS	PERIOD
REHOBOAM		930-913 B.C.
ASA		910-869 B.C.
JEHOSHAPHAT		872-848 B.C.
JEHORAM		853-841 B.C.
ATHALIAH		841-835 B.C.
JOASH		835-796 B.C.
UZZIAH		792-740 B.C.
JOTHAM		750-735 B.C.
AHAZ		735-715 B.C.
HEZEKIAH		715-686 B.C.
	ISAIAH	740-681 B.C.
MANASSEH		697-642 B.C.
JOSIAH		640-609 B.C.
	JEREMIAH	626-585 B.C.
JEHOAHAZ		609 B.C.
JEHOIAKIM		609-598 B.C.
JEHOIACHIN		598-597 B.C.
ZEDEKIAH		597-586 B.C.

END OF SECOND KINGS

THE PROPHETS

EZEKIEL

EZEKIEL THE PRIEST, SON OF BUZI, WAS TAKEN CAPTIVE DURING BABYLON'S SECOND INVASION OF JERUSALEM.

EZEKIEL'S PAD

GURGLE! GURGLE! GURGLE! GURGLE!

GRUMBLE!

GRUMBLE!

WE'RE SUFFERING BECAUSE WE BETRAYED GOD. BUT WHAT SHOULD WE BE DOING HERE? HAS ANYONE HEARD FROM GOD ABOUT THIS SAD STATE OF AFFAIRS?

NOT ME!

EZEKIEL TOOK THE MATTER TO GOD...

GOD, WHAT SHALL THE PEOPLE DO?

GOD!

EZEKIEL! STAND UP AND I WILL SPEAK TO YOU!

I HAVE A MESSAGE FOR YOU TO TAKE TO THE ISRAELITES WHO REBELLED AGAINST ME.

BUT FIRST, EAT THIS!

I'M TO EAT THIS SCROLL? WELL, ALL RIGHT...

YUMMO! THIS TASTES GREAT!

CHOMP! CHOMP!

IS THERE ANY MORE!

MUNCH! MUNCH!

I'M SORRY, GOD! I THOUGHT YOU WANTED ME TO EAT ALL OF IT!

YANK!

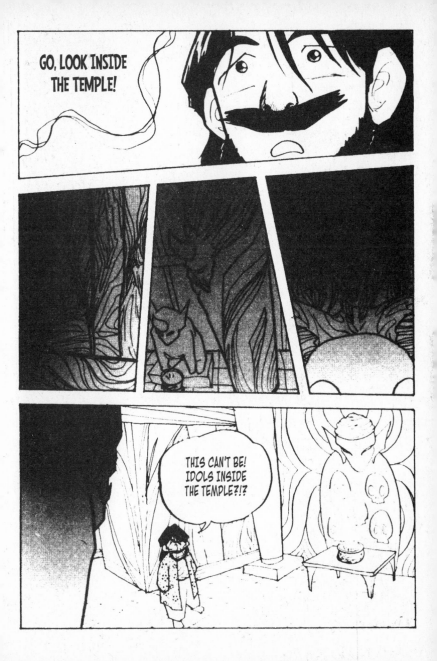

THEY ARE EVEN WORSHIPING THE SUN IN THE COURTYARD.

THEY'RE WORSHIPING IDOLS ALL OVER JERUSALEM!

HOW CAN GOD'S PEOPLE DO SUCH THINGS?

YOU HAVE SEEN THE SINS OF JUDAH. NOW, YOU'LL SEE ITS DESTRUCTION!

I WILL DEAL WITH THEM IN ANGER; I WILL NOT LOOK ON THEM WITH PITY. ALTHOUGH THEY SHOUT IN MY EARS, I WILL NOT LISTEN.

OPERATION WIPEOUT

THE A TEAM

... AND THIS ENDS OUR BRIEFING. IN FIVE MINUTES WE CARRY OUT OPERATION WIPEOUT.

ANGELS ASSEMBLE!

"MARK THE FOLLOWERS OF GOD."

GOD, PLEASE SAVE ME...

A MARK FOR THIS MAN.

NO MARK FOR HIM.

IDOLS, PLEASE SAVE US!

"ANGELS, STRIKE!"

GOD! WILL YOU REALLY DESTROY ISRAEL THAT WAY?

YES! THEIR SINS ARE EXCEEDINGLY GREAT. I WILL BRING DOWN ON THEM WHAT THEY HAVE DONE!

ACCORDING TO GOD'S WILL, JUDAH WAS DESTROYED IN 586 B.C.

CAN THESE BONES COME BACK TO LIFE?

LORD, ONLY YOU KNOW.

TELL THEM TO RETURN TO LIFE.

GOD SAYS FOR YOU TO COME BACK TO LIFE!

CRE-E-EAK!

TH-THEY'RE BECOMING A POWERFUL ARMY!

EZEKIEL, THESE BONES ARE LIKE THE HOUSE OF ISRAEL.

IF THEY WILL PUT THEIR TRUST IN ME, I WILL PUT MY SPIRIT IN THEM AND WILL RETURN THEM TO THEIR LAND.

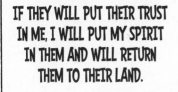

PRAISE YOU, GOD. THERE IS HOPE FOR US.

END OF EZEKIEL

DANIEL

DANIEL WAS ONE OF MANY PRISONERS TAKEN DURING THE FIRST INVASION BY BABYLON.

KING NEBUCHADNEZZAR

YOU BOYS FROM JUDAH, TELL ME YOUR NAMES.

I AM DANIEL.

HANANIAH.

MISHAEL.

AZARIAH.

I AM ASHPENAZ!

I ASKED FOR THE **BOYS'** NAMES, NOT YOURS!

YOU BOYS WILL STUDY FOR THREE YEARS, THEN YOU'LL BE MY SERVANTS.

AND CHAMBERLAIN ASHPENAZ, GIVE THEM BABYLONIAN CLOTHES, BABYLONIAN NAMES, AND PLENTY OF MEAT AND WINE.

YES, MY KING!

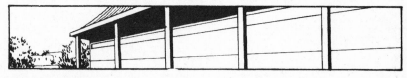

BELTESHAZZAR!

SHADRACH!

MESHACH!

ABEDNEGO!

NOW THAT YOU HAVE BABYLONIAN NAMES, PLEASE ENJOY THE FINEST OF OUR MEATS AND WINES.

PLEASE... EAT ALL YOU WANT!

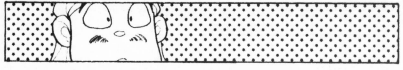

SO SAD, THEY MUST NOT EVEN KNOW HOW TO EAT. THEY'RE ONLY STARING AT THE FOOD.

YOU WHAT!?!

I TOLD YOU TO FEED THEM WELL! THEY LOOK LIKE SCRAWNY MALE MODELS!

THEY JUST WANTED VEGGIES...

I DON'T CARE! YOU DISOBEYED ME, NOW YOU SUFFER!

NO WAY!

YOU WILL STARVE ONLY EATING GRASS!

NO, SIR! WE WON'T BECOME WEAK BY ONLY EATING VEGETABLES!

WHAT? DO YOU WANT TO BE JUST LIKE MALE MODELS?

NOT AT ALL, SIR. BUT IF YOU WILL ALLOW US TO ONLY EAT VEGGIES AND DRINK WATER, YOU CAN COMPARE US TO THE OTHER BOYS. IF WE'RE WEAKER THAN THEY ARE AFTER TEN DAYS, WE'LL EAT MEAT AS YOU WISH.

AFTER TEN DAYS

DANIEL

HANANIAH

MISHAEL

ASHPENAZ CRYING TEARS OF RELIEF.

I USED TO LOOK LIKE THAT, THEN I WENT ON A SEE-FOOD DIET. I SEE IT, I EAT IT.

THIS WAITRESS REMEMBERS BACK WHEN I WAS A STUD.

DID YOU SAY STUD OR DUD?

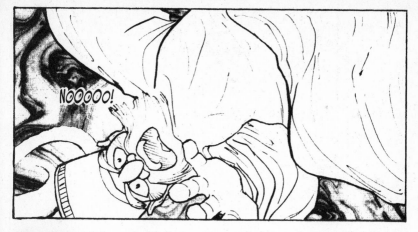

NOOOOO!

BOING!

WHEW! IT WAS A DREAM, JUST A SCARY DREAM!

BUT WHAT COULD IT POSSIBLY MEAN?

FORTUNETELLER

I CAN INTERPRET ANY DREAM.

BUT...

TELL ME WHAT I DREAMT AND TELL ME THE MEANING -- OR YOU DIE!

WHAT!?!

HOW CAN I INTERPRET A DREAM THAT YOU DON'T EVEN REMEMBER?

WAIT, SOLDIER! THINK ABOUT IT! HOW CAN I INTERPRET SUCH A DREAM?!?

ME DON'T THINK. ME JUST DO.

YOU NOT KNOW DREAM? YOU NOT KNOW WHAT IT MEAN?

YES, SO...?

THEN ME KILL YOU!

NO!!!

DANIEL, WE'RE IN TROUBLE!

THE SOLDIER WHO'S KILLING FORTUNETELLERS AND SHAMANS IS COMING TO SEE US!

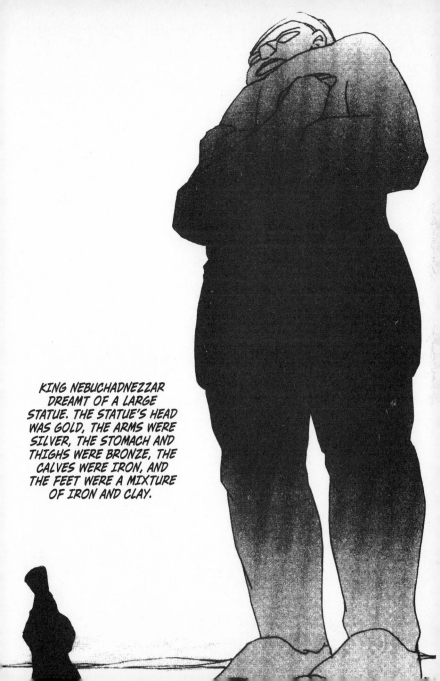

KING NEBUCHADNEZZAR DREAMT OF A LARGE STATUE. THE STATUE'S HEAD WAS GOLD, THE ARMS WERE SILVER, THE STOMACH AND THIGHS WERE BRONZE, THE CALVES WERE IRON, AND THE FEET WERE A MIXTURE OF IRON AND CLAY.

THEN A HUGE ROCK CAME
CRASHING DOWN ...

IT STRUCK THE FEET
AND BROKE THE
STATUE!

KRAKOOM!!

THAT WAS IT! EVERY LAST DETAIL!!!

SO, TELL ME, WHAT DOES IT MEAN?

YOU, MY KING, ARE THE HEAD OF GOLD.
ANOTHER KINGDOM, ONE INFERIOR TO YOURS,
WILL TAKE YOUR PLACE.
THEN A THIRD KINGDOM, ONE OF BRONZE, WILL
RULE OVER THE WHOLE EARTH.
FINALLY A FOURTH KINGDOM, ONE THAT IS STRONG
AS IRON, WILL COME ALONG AND CRUSH AND
SUBDUE ALL THE OTHERS.
THE FEET AND TOES ARE A DIVIDED KINGDOM.
THIS KINGDOM WILL BE PARTLY STRONG AND PARTLY
FRAGILE. THEY WILL SEAL THEIR ALLIANCES BY
INTERMARRIAGE, BUT THEY WILL NEVER BE WHOLLY UNITED.

A : GOLD HEAD

B : CHEST AND ARMS MADE OF SILVER

C : BRONZE STOMACH AND THIGHS

D : IRON CALVES

E : FEET MADE OF IRON AND CLAY

THE GOD OF HEAVEN WILL SET UP A KINGDOM THAT WILL NEVER BE DESTROYED. IT WILL SHATTER ALL THESE KINGDOMS AND BRING THEM TO AN END.

I CAN'T BELIEVE IT, I AM THE HEAD OF GOLD!

THIS GOD YOU SERVE IS THE GOD OF ALL GODS! YOU SHALL BE THE PRIME MINISTER OF MY COUNTRY, AND YOUR FRIENDS SHALL BE GOVERNORS.

THAT'S HOW DANIEL BECAME THE PRIME MINISTER OF BABYLON AND HIS FRIENDS BECAME RULERS OF THE PROVINCES.

LATER, NEBUCHADNEZZAR CONQUERED JERUSALEM AND HE BECAME FULL OF HIMSELF.

VICTORIOUS

ARROGANT

SELF-ABSORBED

VICTORIOUS

ARROGANT

SELF-ABSORBED

BUILD A GOLDEN STATUE IN MY IMAGE FOR THE PEOPLE TO BOW DOWN TO.

AND IF ANYONE DOESN'T BOW DOWN, THEY WILL BE THROWN INTO A FIERY FURNACE!

ONE OF THOSE GOLDEN FINGERS COULD FEED MY FAMILY FOR LIFE.

I WOULDN'T MIND EVEN A GOLDEN TOE...

I'LL SETTLE FOR A WALLET ANY DAY.

THIS IS RIDICULOUS.

PICKPOCKET

I SAID, LET'S ALL BOW DOWN! EVEN YOU THREE!!!

BRING THEM HERE!!!

MY KING, YOU KNOW WE WON'T BOW TO ANYONE BUT GOD.

SHADRACH, MESHACH, ABEDNEGO -- I MADE YOU GOVERNORS OF MY KINGDOM, AND THIS IS HOW YOU REPAY ME?!?

THROW THEM INTO THAT FURNACE!

CRANK IT UP SEVEN TIMES HOTTER THAN USUAL, THEN TOSS 'EM IN!

HURRY IT UP!

THIS CAN'T BE! THEY'RE ALIVE AND WALKING WITH SOMEONE WHO LOOKS LIKE THE SON OF GOD!

SHADRACH, MESHACH, ABEDNEGO! COME OUT OF THERE!!!

WHEN THEY CAME OUT OF THE FIRE UNHARMED, NEBUCHADNEZZAR PROMOTED THEM AND ISSUED A DECREE THAT THOSE WHO BLASPHEMED GOD WOULD BE PUNISHED.

INTERESTED IN TAKING OVER?

I'M A BURN VICTIM, NOT A MUMMY! HOW CAN I DRAW LIKE THIS?

SADLY, NEBUCHADNEZZAR GREW EVEN MORE PRIDEFUL AFTER WINNING MORE BATTLES AND MAKING BABYLON THE MOST POWERFUL NATION IN THE WORLD.

AM I A MAN...

... OR A GOD!?!

AH, THE GREATNESS I HAVE! SUCH STRENGTH! SO HANDSOME! HIGHLY EDUCATED! CHARISMATIC!

YES, I AM NOT HUMAN! I AM A GOD WHO RULES THE HUMAN WORLD!

ANOTHER DREAM!
A TREE GROWING SO
TALL IT TOUCHES
THE SKY!

ALL KINDS OF ANIMALS ARE EATING
ITS FRUITS AND ITS SHADE IS
COVERING THE ENTIRE LAND!

BUT WAIT... AN ANGEL!

LISTEN TO MY WORDS! CUT THE TREE DOWN, LET THE LEAVES AND FRUIT FALL, AND MAKE THE ANIMALS LEAVE!

TIE THE STUMP UP WITH STEEL CHAIN AND LEAVE IT IN THE FOREST FOR SEVEN YEARS!

ANOTHER STRANGE DREAM...

I MUST DISCOVER WHAT IT MEANS!

I DON'T KNOW. MAYBE YOU'RE SUPPOSED TO SAVE THE RAINFORESTS...

I THINK THE NUMBER SEVEN HAS SOMETHING TO DO WITH THE "007" MOVIES OR MAYBE "THE MAGNIFICENT SEVEN"...

I DON'T KNOW WHY YOU'RE ASKING ME. I'M JUST A MANGA ARTIST. I MEAN, I'VE READ THE SCRIPT, BUT I CAN'T TELL YOU WHAT THAT SAYS. THAT WOULD BE LIKE CHEATING!

HE REALLY DIDN'T READ THE SCRIPT EITHER. DON'T LET HIM FOOL YOU.

MANGA BIBLE

ENOUGH!

ENOUGH!!!

THEY ARE ALL USELESS. BRING ME DANIEL!

A TREE? HMM... VERY INTERESTING.

I'M AFRAID TO TELL YOU THOUGH.

COME ON! THE SUSPENSE IS KILLING ME. I WON'T PUNISH YOU -- JUST TELL ME!

OKAY, OKAY...

YOU, MY KING, ARE THE TREE. ALTHOUGH YOUR KINGDOM COVERS THE WORLD, SINCE YOU DENY THAT GOD GAVE YOUR POWER TO YOU, YOU WILL LEAVE YOUR THRONE AND LIVE LIKE A WILD ANIMAL FOR SEVEN YEARS.

AFTER THE SEVEN YEARS, YOU WILL ACKNOWLEDGE THAT GOD GAVE YOU THE POWER AND YOU WILL BECOME KING ONCE MORE.

ONE YEAR LATER...

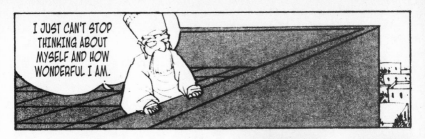

MANY YEARS LATER, BELSHAZZAR BECAME THE LAST KING OF BABYLON.

KING B'S PLACE IS ALWAYS ROCKIN'.

I'M BELSHAZZAR, AND I LIKE TO PAR-TAY!

BY THIS TIME DANIEL HAD BECOME AN OLD MAN.

THE WHITE BEARD MIGHT THROW YOU OFF, BUT YES, I'M DANIEL.

ONE DAY KING BELSHAZZAR WAS THROWING A LARGE PARTY...

EVERY-BODY WANTS TO RULE THE WORRRLD!

I ALWAYS DRINK FROM THE SAME CUP. I NEED A CHANGE!

BRING ME THOSE GOLD AND SILVER CUPS FROM THE TEMPLE OF JERUSALEM!

OH YEAH!

NOW THAT'S SOME BLING!

WHA-WHA-WHA-WHAT? A FLYING HAND IS WRITING SOMETHING ON THE WALL?

WHA-WHAT DOES IT SAY? WHO CAN INTERPRET THESE WORDS?

WELL, LET ME SEE...

NOD

NOD

WELL, WHAT DO THEY MEAN?

THEY AREN'T REAL LETTERS! I COULDN'T EVEN GUESS!

WHY YOU!!!

STALE COOKIE

DIE! DIE!

CALM DOWN!

MY KING, WHY DON'T YOU JUST ASK DANIEL?

AH YES, DANIEL!

MENE, MENE, TEKEL, PARSIN!

BECAUSE YOU DRANK WINE FROM THE CUPS USED IN THE TEMPLE, GOD WILL TAKE YOUR POWER AWAY.

OH, I FORGOT TO MENTION THE KING SAID WHOEVER INTERPRETED THE LETTERS ON THE WALL WOULD BE MADE THIRD HIGHEST IN THE GOVERNMENT.

TOO MUCH PARTYING

LATER THAT EVENING, THE MEDES AND THE PERSIANS JOINED TOGETHER AND INVADED BABYLON, KILLING KING BELSHAZZAR.

DARIUS BECAME KING OF THE NEW COUNTRY MEDE-PERSIA...

FORGET DARIUS, I SHOULD BE KING.

I NEED YOUR WISDOM, DANIEL. PLEASE BE MY PRIME MINISTER.

SURE! BEEN THERE, DONE THAT.

DANIEL BECAME ONE OF THE NEW RULERS AND TAUGHT THE KING WISDOM.

THREE TIMES THREE?

NINE.

SO WISE! I'LL MAKE DANIEL MY SECOND IN COMMAND!

I CAN'T BELIEVE IT!

WHY DO I HAVE TO WORK UNDER A GUY FROM JUDAH!

IS THERE ANY WAY WE CAN GET RID OF DANIEL?

YES! THERE **IS** A WAY!

YOU SCARED ME.

I DIDN'T FLINCH.

DANIEL PRAYS THREE TIMES A DAY BY A WINDOW FACING THE TEMPLE IN JERUSALEM.

A NEW DECREE?

YES! YOU MUST DECREE THAT FOR THE NEXT THIRTY DAYS NO ONE IS TO PRAY TO ANY OTHER GODS. THEY CAN ONLY PRAY TO YOU, YOUR HIGHNESS.

AND IF ANYONE DISOBEYS THE DECREE, THEY SHOULD BE THROWN INTO THE LIONS' DEN.

NOT BAD! SOUNDS GOOD - TO ME!

WHAT DOES IT SAY? I CAN'T READ...

ANNOUNCEMENT -- FOR THIRTY DAYS YOU MUST ONLY PRAY TO THE KING! THOSE WHO DISOBEY WILL BE LION CHOW. - KING DARIUS

THE NEXT MORNING...

DANIEL!
DANIEL!

DANIEL! ARE YOU DEAD?

NO, MY KING!
GOD CLOSED THE
MOUTH OF THE LIONS
AND SAVED ME.

DANIEL!

MY KING.

PUT THE MEN WHO ACCUSED DANIEL IN THE LIONS' DEN!

AFTER THIS, DANIEL WAS LOVED BY THE KING AND RULED THE WHOLE COUNTRY.

END OF DANIEL

ESTHER

THIS IS THE STORY OF ESTHER, THE MOST BEAUTIFUL WOMAN IN ALL OF PERSIA. I CAN'T BELIEVE I ONLY GET TO DRAW ONE SIDE OF HER HEAD. I QUIT!

IT TOOK MORE THAN TEN HOURS FOR ME TO DRAW THAT.

WHAT? THE ARTIST IS QUITTING?!?

PUBLISHER

HOORAY! HOORAY!

GOOD TIMES!!

ARTIST TO CHANGE! BOOK OF ESTHER EXPECTED TO BE BESTSELLER NOW!

CELEBRATION BEGINS!

THE CARTOONIST WHO WAS CONSIDERED THE MAIN REASON FOR THE LOW SALES OF THE MANGA BIBLE HAS ANNOUNCED HIS RESIGNATION! THE SERIES IS NOW EXPECTED TO EXPERIENCE AN INCREASE IN SALES...

SOMETIMES...

... A PERSON'S DECISION, HOWEVER SANE IT SEEMED...

... MAY CHANGE!

ALL RIGHT! IS THERE ANYBODY ELSE WHO DOESN'T WANT ME BACK?!?

ESTHER LOST HER PARENTS AT A YOUNG AGE, SO SHE WAS RAISED BY HER COUSIN MORDECAI.

BOO HOO!

DON'T WORRY, LITTLE ESTHER. I WILL RAISE YOU INTO A WONDERFUL WOMAN.

IN PERSIA'S CITADEL OF SUSA...

... A GREAT FEAST WAS HELD ...

... BY KING XERXES.

THIS PARTY IS AWESOME! DON'T YOU ALL AGREE?

TELL QUEEN VASHTI TO COME OUT AND SHOW HER BEAUTY!

THAT'S WHAT I'M TALKING ABOUT!

IT WILL BE MY FIRST TIME TO SEE THE QUEEN!

WHAT? AM I JUST A SHOWGIRL? FORGET IT! I'M NOT GOING OVER THERE!

WHAT? SHE REFUSES TO COME!?!

HOW DARE SHE DISOBEY HER KING -- HER HUSBAND!

I KNOW SHE'S A QUEEN, BUT HER HUSBAND NEEDS TO SHOW HER WHO THE BOSS IS!

I WISH I HAD A WIFE!

IF MY WIFE HEARS ABOUT THIS, SHE'LL THINK IT'S VERY FUNNY.

TELL VASHTI THAT SHE IS **BANISHED** FROM MY PRESENCE! PROCLAIM THROUGHOUT THE LAND THAT **ALL WOMEN ARE TO RESPECT THEIR HUSBANDS!** I WILL SEEK OUT A NEW QUEEN!

SO WOMEN CAME FROM ACROSS THE COUNTRY TO APPLY TO BE THE NEW QUEEN.

YES! THIS IS WHAT I'VE SCULPTED MY BEAUTIFUL BODY FOR!

THE KING NEEDS SOMEONE SUPER.

OH YEAH? WELL HE'S THE WIND BENEATH MY WINGS!

DON'T START THE ROSE CEREMONY WITHOUT ME!

YOU WANT ME TO GO?

YES, ESTHER. IF GOD HELPS US, YOU WILL BE QUEEN!

BUT THEY WILL KICK ME OUT SINCE I'M A JEW.

THEN YOU MUST HIDE THAT FACT.

BE CAREFUL!

OUR PEOPLE ARE JUST FOREIGNERS HERE. WE ARE NOT TRULY SAFE.

IF YOU ARE CHOSEN AS A QUEEN, YOU WILL BE ABLE TO HELP OUR PEOPLE.

YOU'RE RIGHT. PLEASE PRAY FOR ME.

AT THE PALACE...

I WILL STUN HIM WITH MY BEAUTY!

OR STUN HIM WITH YOUR APPETITE.

I FEEL LIKE I'M ON THE BACHELOR TV SHOW!

THERE WERE MANY BEAUTIFUL WOMEN, BUT ESTHER WAS THE ONLY ONE HE NOTICED.

ESTHER BECAME THE QUEEN -- AND YET ANOTHER WOMAN GOT AWAY FROM ME.

OH YEAH! I FORGOT TO MENTION -- MORDECAI WAS ALSO A HIGH OFFICIAL IN PERSIA.

IT'S A RELIEF THAT ESTHER BECAME A QUEEN.

PSST! PSST! PSST! PSST!

WHO COULD THAT BE?

I CAN'T STAND IT ANYMORE. LET'S KILL THE KING!

YEAH! LET'S TURN THIS COUNTRY UPSIDE-DOWN!

WHAT? THOSE ARE THE COURT OFFICIALS BIGTHANA AND TERESH! WHAT ARE THEY TALKING ABOUT...?

LET'S DO IT ON...

NO, THAT'S MY BIRTHDAY.

QUEEN ESTHER, TWO COURT OFFICIALS ARE PLANNING ON KILLING THE KING...

KING! ACCORDING TO MORDECAI, THERE IS A PLOT TO KILL YOU...

HOW DARE YOU!?! EXECUTE THEM!!!

THOSE MEDDLING KIDS!

WHEW! I'M SO GLAD I LEARNED OF THE PLOT TO KILL ME.

IF IT WASN'T FOR THEM...!

I MUST WRITE IN MY DIARY ABOUT HOW MORDECAI SAVED ME.

OUT OF THE WAY! HERE COMES THE NEW PRIME MINISTER, HAMAN!

ON YOUR KNEES TO PAY TRIBUTE TO THE GREAT HAMAN!

WHO IS THAT?

I AM A JEW.

SO WHAT? BOW DOWN AND PAY TRIBUTE TO THE NEW PRIME MINISTER!

I SERVE GOD! I CANNOT AND WILL NOT BOW DOWN TO A HUMAN.

OH, MORDECAI, MY JEWISH FRIEND, HAVE I GOT PLANS FOR YOU...

SO, THERE ARE PEOPLE IN MY KINGDOM WHO DISOBEY THE LAWS I CREATE?

YES, MY KING! THEY LIVE ACCORDING TO THEIR LAWS AND NOT TO YOURS.

ALL RIGHT! WHO ARE THEY?

THEY ARE THE JEWS, MY KING. THEY ONLY WORSHIP THEIR GOD AND CAUSE PROBLEMS ALL THE TIME.

I CAN SET ASIDE TEN THOUSAND TALENTS OF SILVER IN ORDER TO TAKE CARE OF THIS JEWISH PROBLEM.

TEN THOUSAND? VERY GOOD. HERE'S MY RING. DO AS YOU LIKE!

NOOO!!!

GOD, PLEASE DON'T ABANDON US!

WHEN THE KING'S DECREE -- ARRANGED BY HAMAN -- SPREAD THROUGHOUT THE COUNTRY, ALL THE JEWS PUT ON SACKCLOTH AND ASHES AND WEPT IN PRAYER WHILE FASTING.

WHAT!?! MY COUSIN IS WEEPING IN RAGS AT THE KING'S GATE?

YES, MA'AM. I SAW IT MYSELF.

PLEASE, SEND HIM NICE NEW CLOTHES.

HE WOULDN'T TAKE THEM?

NO, MA'AM. HE SAYS HE WANTS YOU TO PLEAD WITH THE KING BEFORE ALL THE JEWS ARE KILLED.

WHAT ARE YOU TALKING ABOUT?

IF YOU DIDN'T KNOW, MORDECAI SAID YOU SHOULD TURN BACK TWO PAGES AND SEE FOR YOURSELF.

BACK THERE? OH...THAT'S WHAT HAPPENED! I HAVE TO PAY ATTENTION EVEN WHEN I'M NOT APPEARING.

BUT, I CAN'T GO TO THE KING UNLESS HE CALLS ME. THE LAW SAYS ANYONE WHO ENTERS THE COURT WITHOUT PERMISSION IS KILLED.

THE ONLY WAY THEY'D LIVE IS IF THE KING POINTED HIS SCEPTER AT THEM. USUALLY THEY DIED.

ANYHOO, MORDECAI KNEW QUEEN ESTHER WOULD BE WORRIED, SO HE SENT HER A LETTER.

ESTHER, GOD MADE YOU A QUEEN FOR SUCH A TIME AS THIS! DON'T THINK YOU WILL ESCAPE ONCE THEY BEGIN TO ATTACK THE JEWS. IF YOU DON'T HELP, GOD WILL SAVE US ANOTHER WAY, BUT YOU WILL PERISH.

COUSIN, I WILL RISK MY LIFE AND SEEK THE KING'S FAVOR. GATHER THE JEWS AND WE SHOULD ALL FAST AND PRAY FOR THREE DAYS. THEN I WILL GO TO THE KING, AND IF I DIE... I DIE.

AFTER THREE DAYS, ESTHER ENTERED THE PALACE. SHE LOOKED EVEN MORE RADIANT AND BEAUTIFUL AFTER THREE DAYS OF PRAYING.

ESTHER, MY BEAUTIFUL BRIDE, HERE IS MY SCEPTER, PLEASE COME NEAR. NOW TELL ME, WHY HAVE YOU COME?

I'VE PREPARED A FEAST FOR YOU AND THE LOYAL HAMAN. PLEASE JOIN ME.

DURING THE FEAST

THE QUEEN INVITED ME WITH THE KING... I'M THE MAN!

NOW, TELL ME, ESTHER, WHAT CAN I DO FOR YOU? I WOULD GIVE YOU HALF THE COUNTRY, IF YOU'D LIKE.

I'LL ASK YOU TOMORROW, IF YOU AND HAMAN WILL JOIN ME FOR DINNER AGAIN.

MUNCH MUNCH MUNCH

I'M INVITED TO ANOTHER FEAST TOMORROW! I CAN'T STAND MYSELF!

HUH!?!

SO, MORDECAI STILL WON'T BOW IN MY PRESENCE! I'LL TAKE CARE OF HIM.

WHY DO WE HAVE A TELEPHONE POLE?

IT'S NOT A TELEPHONE POLE! I'M GONNA KILL MORDECAI BY HANGING HIM ON IT!

THAT NIGHT...

I CAN'T SLEEP. HMMM, I HAVEN'T READ MY DIARY IN A LONG TIME!

NOW, I'M GETTING SLEEPY...

MORDECAI SAVED MY LIFE, BUT WHAT DID I DO FOR HIM...?

I CAN'T LET HIS DEED GO UNNOTICED! I'LL REWARD HIM TOMORROW!

REWARD?

REWARD!?!

YES, I WANT TO REWARD A GOOD SERVANT. WHAT SHOULD I DO?

HE'S TALKING ABOUT ME, I KNOW IT! I KNOW IT!!!

HMM... WHAT WOULD I WANT?

OKAY! THE SERVANT SHOULD BE GIVEN THE KING'S CROWN AND ROBES TO WEAR, HE SHOULD RIDE THE KING'S HORSE, AND HAVE A HIGH OFFICIAL PARADE HIM THROUGH THE CITY, TELLING ALL HIS GOOD DEEDS.

GREAT! DO EVERYTHING YOU JUST SAID FOR MORDECAI, THE FAITHFUL SERVANT WHO SAVED MY LIFE!

THIS IS MORDECAI WHO SAVED THE KING. WHOOPEE DOO-DAH...

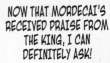

NOW THAT MORDECAI'S RECEIVED PRAISE FROM THE KING, I CAN DEFINITELY ASK!

SO, ESTHER, PLEASE TELL ME YOUR WISH.

I LOST MY APPETITE.

THIS IS DIFFICULT...

SOMEONE IS TRYING TO KILL MY PEOPLE.

WHO IS THIS FIEND?!?

THE FIEND IS HAMAN.

SHE MUST BE A JEW, BUT I HAD NO IDEA...

SPARE ME!

NO, MY QUEEN! NO!!!

SPARE ME!

GET YOUR HANDS OFF HER! TAKE THIS FILTHY SLIME-BUCKET AWAY!

NO, NO... THIS IS ALL WRONG...

I KNOW, I KNOW -- HE CAN DISH IT OUT, BUT HE CAN'T TAKE IT.

HAMAN WAS HUNG ON THE TELEPHONE POLE HE PREPARED FOR MORDECAI.

IT'S NOT A TELEPHONE POLE!

NOW THE PROBLEM WITH HAMAN'S DECREE IS THAT IT HAD THE KING'S SEAL, SO IT WAS A LAW.

HOWEVER, THE KING GRANTED MORDECAI HIS RING WHICH WOULD SOLVE THE PROBLEM...

WITH THE KING'S RING, MORDECAI ISSUED A NEW DECREE, STATING THAT ALL JEWS COULD KILL ANYONE WHO ATTACKED THEM.

FINALLY, ALL THE JEWS GATHERED TOGETHER AND DEFENDED THEMSELVES AGAINST THEIR ATTACKERS. IN REMEMBRANCE OF GOD'S PROTECTION DURING THIS TIME, THE JEWS HAD A SPECIAL CELEBRATION FEAST CALLED PURIM, AND IT WAS TO BE HELD THE SAME TIME EVERY YEAR THEREAFTER.

KING XERXES PROMOTED MORDECAI TO THE SECOND IN COMMAND IN ALL OF PERSIA, AND ESTHER WAS LOVED BY THE KING AND THE PEOPLE.

END OF ESTHER

EZRA & NEHEMIAH

IN 539 B.C., KING CYRUS OF PERSIA DESTROYED BABYLON.

CALL THE JEWISH LEADERS: ZERUBBABEL, JESHUA, AND ALL THE REST!

THE ARTIST WAS DRAWING THIS AT CHRISTMASTIME AND HAD OTHER THINGS ON HIS MIND.

HERE THEY ARE!

I, KING CYRUS, WHO CONQUERED THIS LAND BY GOD'S GRACE, AM LETTING YOU RETURN TO JERUSALEM TO REBUILD GOD'S TEMPLE! I'M ALSO RETURNING THE GOLD BABYLON TOOK FROM YOUR PEOPLE AS WELL AS GIVING YOU PLENTY OF GIFTS TO USE FOR THE WORK! HO HO HO!

OVER FORTY THOUSAND JEWS LEFT FOR JERUSALEM FROM THEIR EXILE IN BABYLON. HOWEVER, WHEN THEY ARRIVED...

NO! IT'S TOTALLY GONE!

WHERE THE TEMPLE USED TO BE.

ONCE THEY SETTLED BACK IN THEIR HOMES, THEY BUILT AN ALTAR AND GAVE A BURNT OFFERING TO GOD.

SNIFF! SNIFF!

OOOOH! OOOOH!!

KING ARTAXERXES ORDERED THAT THE BUILDING OF THE TEMPLE MUST STOP. SO THE JEWS GOT BUSY BUILDING THEIR OWN HOMES.

BY THE COMMAND OF KING ARTAXERXES, ALL JEWS ARE TO STOP THE TEMPLE CONSTRUCTION IMMEDIATELY!

IT'S BEEN TEN YEARS...

RUMBLE!

GRUMBLE!

GURGLE!

SCRAPE! SCRAPE!

STOP SCRAPING THE CONTAINER, HONEY. THERE'S NO MORE FOOD.

WHY HAS THIS FAMINE COME UPON US?

I'M SO HUNGRY I CAN'T EVEN THINK.

FEED ME!

FEED ME!

PEOPLE OF JERUSALEM!

PROPHET HAGGAI

LISTEN UP!

PROPHET ZECHARIAH

CYRUS, THE GRANDFATHER OF THE NEW KING DARIUS, COMMANDED US TO BUILD IT.

WHAT? KING CYRUS?!?

I'LL CONFIRM THIS! IF YOU LIE, YOU DIE!

THE DECREE BY THE KING CYRUS WAS CONFIRMED AND THE TEMPLE WAS FINALLY COMPLETED IN 516 B.C.

ANYTHING ELSE I CAN HELP WITH?

NOPE! WE'RE GOOD!

DURING THE REIGN OF KING ARTAXERXES IN PERSIA...

I WANNA GO HOME TO JERUSA-LOME! JERUSA-LOME! JERUSA-LOME!!

HEY! CUT THAT RACKET OUT!

YES! I'LL GO HOME TO JERUSALEM... INSTEAD OF JUST SINGING ABOUT IT!

EZRA, A JEWISH PRIEST WHO HOLDS A HIGH POSITION IN BABYLON.

JERUSA-LOME!

OH, EZRA! I'M SAD TO SEE YOU GO, BUT IF YOU MUST -- YOU MUST.

MELLOWED WITH AGE.

GO, TAKE YOUR FRIENDS WITH YOU AND BRING TREASURE FOR GOD.

MY ARMY WILL PROTECT YOU ON YOUR JOURNEY.

THANKS, KING!

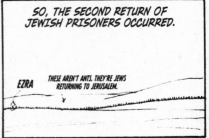

SO, THE SECOND RETURN OF JEWISH PRISONERS OCCURRED.

EZRA

THESE AREN'T ANTS. THEY'RE JEWS RETURNING TO JERUSALEM.

BUT WHEN THEY REACHED JERUSALEM...

OH NO!

ANYTHING GOES

ILLEGAL MARRIAGE SERVICE & IDOL WORSHIPING SCHOOL

NO! NO! NOOO!!!

HOW CAN YOU ANGER GOD BY MARRYING GENTILES AND WORSHIPING IDOLS AFTER ALL THOSE YEARS OF EXILE?!?

STOP THIS INSANITY!

SO THE ISRAELITES DIVORCED THE GENTILE WOMEN, AND EZRA'S REVOLUTION BEGAN.

AFTER HEARING ABOUT THE SAD STATE OF JERUSALEM, NEHEMIAH DIDN'T EAT FOR DAYS AND HE PRAYED WITH TEARS...

GOD! SEND ME TO JERUSALEM TO BUILD THE CITY AGAIN!

WHAT'S GOING ON HERE?!?

WHAT'S THE MATTER, NEHEMIAH?

JERUSALEM, WHERE MY FOREFATHERS ARE BURIED, LIES IN RUIN. HOW CAN I LIVE IN SUCH LUXURY?

I'D LIKE TO GO BACK AND REBUILD THE CITY WALL.

I AM SAD TO SEE YOU GO... BUT ALL RIGHT.

I WILL ALSO SEND ALONG SOLDIERS AND SUPPLIES TO HELP YOU REBUILD THE CITY WALL!

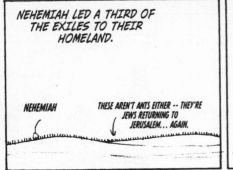

LET'S BRIBE SOMEONE TO GET NEHEMIAH OUTSIDE ALONE...AND KILL HIM!

NEHEMIAH! THEY'RE TRYING TO KILL YOU. YOU MUST HIDE IN THE TEMPLE!

I WILL NOT HIDE IN THE TEMPLE JUST TO SAVE MY LIFE. IT'S A SIN SINCE I'M NOT A PRIEST. GOD WILL PROTECT ME.

WE... GIVE... UP!

DESPITE OF ALL THE INTERFERENCE, NEHEMIAH WAS ABLE TO REBUILD THE WALL OF JERUSALEM AND PROVIDE THE JEWISH PEOPLE WITH A SECURE PLACE TO LIVE AND WORSHIP GOD.

END OF EZRA & NEHEMIAH

CHECK OUT THESE OTHER Z GRAPHIC NOVELS!

I Was an Eighth-Grade Ninja
Available Now!

The Judge of God
Available Now!

Pyramid Peril
Available Now!

The Coming Storm
Available Now!

Advent
Available Now!

ZONDERVAN®

We want to hear from you. Please send your comments
about this book to us in care of zreview@zondervan.com. Thank you.

Grand Rapids, MI 49530
www.zonderkidz.com

ZONDERVAN.com/
AUTHORTRACKER
follow your favorite authors

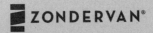